Samuel French Acting Edition

Twelve Dancing Princesses

Adapted by Richard Hellesen

Please refer to page 58 for further copyright information.

CHARACTERS

A YOUNG MAN [MICHAEL]
A MYSTERIOUS OLD WOMAN, Who Appears
   in a Variety of Guises Throughout
THE TWELVE PRINCESSES:
    [ASHLEY,
       CHELSEA,
           HOLLY,
            JESSI,
               JILL,
                 LILY,
                   LINDSAY,
                     LUCY,
                       MORGAN,
                         NICOLE,
                           SHANNON,
                            and SARAH]

THE KING, Their Father
TWO SERVANTS

TIME

Once Upon A Time

PLACE

In A Faraway Land

This adaptation of THE TWELVE DANCING PRINCESSES was first produced by the Young Conservatory Players of South Coast Repertory, David Emmes and Martin Benson, Artistic Directors, December 14-23, 1990, with the following cast:

The King...Gare Mattison
Ashley...Marijen Gorska
Chelsea................................... Melany Anne Linder
Holly...Susan Ihrke
Jessi... Amy E. Turner
Jill...Treva Lanphier
Lily... Erika Hickey
Lindsay...Erin Hickey
Lucy...Cindy Alberts
Morgan...Laura Escalante
Nicole...Melanie A. Wingo
Shannon...Jennie Sheffield
Sarah...Kate Staiger
Michael... Curt Cornelius
Old Woman...Carole Cooney
Servants... Michael Miller,
Matt Singer

Directed by Diane Doyle
Original Music by Richard Jennings
Choreography by Kathy Kahn
Design by Dwight Richard Odle
Stage Manager: Claire Sigman

For Sarah

THE TWELVE DANCING PRINCESSES

or,

The Shoes That Were Danced To Pieces

Scene 1

(Once Upon A Time—late in the morning. A small stand of trees next to a road which winds through A Faraway Land. In the dark, a trumpet fanfare which turns into stately music as the lights come up full. A PROCESSION makes its way across, around, betwixt and between the stage and audience. Two SERVANTS lead the way, perhaps with banners. They are followed by THE TWELVE PRINCESSES—who are as different as different can be, from their variously ornamented gowns down to the soles of their variously colored brand-new dancing shoes. They are followed by THE KING himself - who, in spite of his brilliant crown and ermine robes, seems oddly preoccupied with something. He waves perfunctorily once in awhile. The procession continues, and as it does it conceals the entrance of a YOUNG MAN—a handsome young man wearing un-handsome clothes, who carries with him a tattered satchel and a walking stick. When we finally do catch sight of him, as the procession begins to exit the stage, HE is standing with head bowed slightly.

Bowed, that is, until the last princess—PRINCESS

SARAH—passes him. HE catches sight of her, and SHE glances at him a trifle too long—turning quickly away as his gaze meets hers. He watches, transfixed, as she slowly looks at him again, an expression of wonder and fear on her face. A moment; then the young man remembers who he is and who she is, and bows to her. The music begins to recede in the distance as the two oldest Princesses, ASHLEY and CHELSEA, return. THEY stop short when they see what is happening. CHELSEA isn't sure what to do, but ASHLEY is quite clear on the concept.)

ASHLEY: *(Forcefully.)* Sarah.*(SHE grabs Sarah by the arm and hauls her off. CHELSEA almost says something, but exits silently, after giving the Young Man a bemused look. The music fades in the distance.)*
YOUNG MAN: *(Still watching off.)* "Sarah"... *(Sighs.)* If only the world were different... If only I were different. If I were more than just a wandering laborer...how would you look at me then? *(Picks up his satchel and stick, then turns back in the direction the princesses exited.)* But if *you* were different—if you were less than a princess...I think I could look at you forever.
VOICE: "Forever"?
YOUNG MAN: *(Slight pause.)* Yes.
VOICE: "Forever" is quite a word, young man. Are you sure you want to use it?
YOUNG MAN: *(Looking around.)* Who are you? Where are you? *(What appears to have been a rock unfolds—and A MYSTERIOUS OLD WOMAN stands before the YOUNG MAN. She wears a voluminous hooded cape.)*
OLD WOMAN: Right here, of course.

YOUNG MAN: Where did you come from?

OLD WOMAN: If you can tell me where wishes go, then I can tell you whence I've come.

YOUNG MAN: No-one knows where wishes go.

OLD WOMAN: Then, you have your answer.

YOUNG MAN: (*Pause; smiles*.) All right, old woman. Enough of your riddles. What do you want with me?

OLD WOMAN: I think the question is, rather, what do you want for yourself? Where are you going? And what do you hope to find when you get there?

YOUNG MAN: (*The truth*.) I don't know.

OLD WOMAN: Then perhaps you should go home.

YOUNG MAN: That's just it: I haven't a home. Not really. My parents are dead, our land is gone--I've had to set out through the country to seek my fortune. Only I don't know where to find it. Or what my fortune would be even if I did find it. (*Looking off toward where the procession exited*.) Sometimes I think I catch a glimpse of it...and then I think: no. Some dreams are too great for someone like me.

OLD WOMAN: Ah, but the trick is not, Believing in what you've seen--the trick is, Believing in what you've yet to see. (*Swirling the cape around her, SHE "disappears" again*.)

YOUNG MAN: (*Looking around*.) Where did you go?!

OLD WOMAN: (*"Reappearing" behind him*.) Maybe I can help you.

YOUNG MAN: But...you don't know what I'm seeking, either.

OLD WOMAN: Oh, I think I do. (*Indicates off*.) She's very beautiful, isn't she.

YOUNG MAN: (*Pause*.) Yes. She is. But...it's impossible.

OLD WOMAN: Perhaps not. Surely you've heard of the

impossible.

OLD WOMAN: Perhaps not. Surely you've heard of the Princesses and their shoes.

YOUNG MAN: Their shoes?

OLD WOMAN: Or, maybe you haven't...[*Note: if desired, the following scene could be acted out in pantomime or dance behind, perhaps with incidental music, as the OLD WOMAN describes it.*]

OLD WOMAN: There is a room--in the farthest corner of the farthest tower of the farthest wing of the castle. In this room, there are twelve beds--one for each of the Princesses, for this is where they sleep every night.

YOUNG MAN: In the same room? But the castle is so big--

OLD WOMAN: I know. But the King...well. He's a very protective man. So protective that the single door to the bedroom is locked with triple locks--and he keeps the keys.

YOUNG MAN: He must be very cruel.

OLD WOMAN: (*Somewhat wistfully.*) Not cruel, no. But with twelve daughters to look after by himself...

YOUNG MAN: They've lost their mother, too?

OLD WOMAN: (*Quietly.*) Many years ago. The Queen died giving birth to the youngest Princess.

YOUNG MAN: (*Still looking off.*) Sarah.

OLD WOMAN: (*Tenderly, with a gentle nod.*) Sarah. (*Pause.*) Since that day, as the Princesses have grown, so too has the King's determination that no-one will take them from him. Every night at sunset he himself locks them in. And every morning at sunrise he himself lets them out. Now, here is the mystery. Every morning, when the King unlocks the door, he finds twelve pairs of shoes on the threshold. And every one of them is in pieces--as though they had been worn out with dancing.

YOUNG MAN: But that's impossible.

OLD WOMAN: Like attaining the hand of a princess? And yet it happens. And when the King asks his daughters what they do at night, they answer only, "We sleep, Father." And then they laugh.

YOUNG MAN: (*After a moment.*) What does this have to do with me?

OLD WOMAN: Just this. The King is so desperate to solve the mystery, that he has promised a reward to any man who can discover the secret of the shoes: a princess of the young man's choosing, as his bride.

YOUNG MAN: (*Getting interested in the challenge.*) And no-one has tried to solve it?

OLD WOMAN: Oh, many have tried, but...If the young man has not discovered the secret in three days, he loses his head. (*Pause.*) Now. Is she still as beautiful as you thought she was?

YOUNG MAN: (*Thinks a moment; gazes off, then smiles.*) More. (*Slight pause.*) I think I should like to try.

OLD WOMAN: You might lose.

YOUNG MAN: But I might win.

OLD WOMAN: Either way, it's forever. You understand?

YOUNG MAN: (*Nods.*) Forever.

OLD WOMAN: Then...I think you might find this useful. (*SHE removes her cloak and hands it to him.*) If you wear this, you will become invisible. You can follow the Princesses unseen, and perhaps discover what really happens in the night.

YOUNG MAN: But how can I possibly approach the King? How can I persuade him to give me a chance?

OLD WOMAN: I have heard that the castle gardener is in desperate need of help. I would think he could use a strong

young man like you.
  YOUNG MAN: And what do you want in return?

  OLD WOMAN: When you have what you want, I will have
what I want. (*The YOUNG MAN says nothing, just looks at
the cloak and thinks.*) Trust who you are, and what you know,
and all will be well. (*SHE vanishes.*)
  YOUNG MAN: Wait! What if I'm found out? What if
the magic fails me? What if I can't solve the mystery in three
days? Will you be able to help me? How can I find you? (*A
pause. HE sighs, then looks at the cloak, and turns toward the
castle.*) The hand of a princess... (*HE tosses the cloak over
his shoulder, and walks off. Beautiful, bright music comes up
as the lights fade quickly out, and continues through the scene
change.*)

*

Scene 2

(*The Castle—early afternoon. A throne somewhere on
stage that is not center; a stone bench downstage.*

*The scene change music has been joined by a choir of
VOICES, singing a madrigal. [See Music Notes
following script.] The voices are young, angelic, and—*

as we see when the lights come up—belong to the TWELVE PRINCESSES. They are being conducted in their singing practice by a MUSIC TEACHER, who bears an uncanny resemblance to the Mysterious Old Woman... As the song continues, the KING slips in to watch. The song ends gloriously, and the KING applauds.)

KING: Wonderful! Simply wonderful.

TEACHER: Thank you, Your Majesty.

KING: But with twelve such lovely voices, how could it not be? (*Moving to the Princesses.*) My darlings...my angels... This is how I love to see you spending your time. Together...happy...and that makes me happy.

LILY AND LINDSAY: Thank you, Father.

LUCY: Thank you, sir.

CHELSEA: (*Starts to speak, but then:*)

ASHLEY: It's our duty, of course.

NICOLE: (*Emotional.*) I think it's sooo beautiful...

HOLLY: (*Grinning, to Nicole.*) You would.

JILL: We're not *that* good...

JESSI: I want a solo. How come I don't get...

SHANNON: (*Mocking JESSI, with a giggle.*) "I want a solo, I want a solo"...

MORGAN: It doesn't matter anyway. Nothing matters. (*The PRINCESSES stop and look at MORGAN, then:*)

SARAH: (*To the KING.*) Thank you, Father. We're glad you like it.

KING: I only wish you would spend more time singing— (*Pointedly.*)--and less on your other activities. At least when you sing you share with me, instead of keeping things from me. At least when you sing I know what you're up to. At least when you sing, you don't wear out dozens of pairs of shoes! (*Pause; a studied calmness.*) Please. All I want is an answer.

ASHLEY: (*Mildly.*) An answer to what, Father?

KING: YOU KNOW VERY WELL "TO WHAT"!

ASHLEY: I don't see that it's anyone's business but ours.

KING: Tell that to the gentlemen who are losing their heads around here on a regular basis! (*Pause.*) I demand to know! What is it that you do when you've been locked into your room at night?! (*CHELSEA starts to speak.*)

THE PRINCESSES: We sleep, Father. (*Slight pause; SHANNON giggles, LUCY elbows her.*)

KING: (*Pause; sizing them up, then:*) All right. If that's the way it's going to be...if you mean to fling down the love I have for you and dance on it...fine. I am your father, and fathers--believe it or not--can be hurt. (*Harder.*) But I am also the King--and Kings, believe it you will, must and shall have an answer. (*Scans them all.*) Rehearsal is over. (*HE goes off.*)

TEACHER: (*Following him.*) Your majesty, wait! (*Stops, turns back to the PRINCESSES, and sighs.*) What are we going to do with you... (*Turns and runs off.*) Your majesty! Please... (*A slight pause.*)

LUCY: What are they "going to do" with us? (*Shakes her head at the question.*)

SHANNON: Leave us alone might be nice.

JESSI: (*Preening, admiring her shoes.*) He doesn't understand. He never understands.

HOLLY: Well, he doesn't know what there is to understand, does he.

ASHLEY: And he's never going to know--(*Pointedly.*) Right? (*CHELSEA starts to speak.*)

MORGAN: He'll find out. One of these days.

SHANNON: Morgannnn...

MORGAN: It's true. We're doomed and you know it.

LILY AND LINDSAY: Not if we keep it to ourselves.

NICOLE: Oh, we have to. I mean, we just have to! I don't think I could live if I didn't have it to look forward to... (*She is holding her arms out in front of her, miming dancing.*)

JILL: Well, sure, it's nice, but...it's just so sad to see Father like that.

SARAH: (*Who has been musing.*) Do you think it's true? What he said?

LILY: What about?

LINDSAY: About what?

SARAH: About being hurt.

ASHLEY: (*A laugh.*) Father?

JESSI: Don't be ridiculous.

SARAH: But you know how much he cares for us...

HOLLY: Sure, Sarah. Three locks on the bedroom door--how sweet of him.

LUCY: Not to mention the headless corpses piling up outside.

NICOLE: (*Glumly perching on the throne.*) That is just sooo sad...

MORGAN: (*Flat.*) Depends on how you look at it.

ASHLEY: Sarah...I've known him longer than any of us. And believe me, the last time he was hurt was when Mother died. After that, he locked himself up, inside. He's going to be unhappy, so everyone must be unhappy. But we are not his kingdom--we belong to ourselves. And if that means that we have to discover our own world, and go there, where he cannot follow... (*Smiles slyly.*) Besides, it's a better world than this one, you know it is.

SARAH: Only for a time.

ASHLEY: But it's *our* time. It's fun, and magic, and life.
And we're not going to give it up--no matter what he does.

(*The PRINCESSES set up a chatter of agreement and
disagreement in response--all but SARAH, who stands
silently apart. As they do, the YOUNG MAN appears
at the side of the stage. One by one the PRINCESSES
see him, and falter. THEY exit quickly--except for
SARAH, who smiles faintly at the YOUNG MAN.
Recognizing him, ASHLEY gives him a defiant look,
then takes SARAH's arm and pulls her out. From
another part of the stage, the KING steps in, in time to
catch the last moment. HE sizes up the Young Man,
then speaks.*)

KING: Well. There's no shortage of courage in this
kingdom, is there?
YOUNG MAN: (*Turns and kneels quickly.*) Your
Majesty...
KING: At least I can say that much... (*Eventually works
his way toward the throne; he speaks by rote, as though he has
done this a dozen times--which he has.*) All right. You know
the problem. You clearly know the reward or you wouldn't be
here. You also, I'm certain, know the risks. I'm not happy
about those risks, but there must be rules, mustn't there? We
cannot live in a world without circumscriptions. Rules, my
boy--without them there is disorder, distrust, rampant
unhappiness--and that--do not mistake me--is what I'm about
here: happiness. It's worth a dead prince or two. Or three.
(*With a frown.*) Or more. But we'll worry about that later...
Simply put: I'm offering the hand of one of my daughters--not
something I do lightly, but there it is. What I want from you

is the solution to my problem. (*Slight pause.*) I would also like it if you would stop kneeling. You've made your point.

YOUNG MAN: (*Rising.*) Yes, Majesty.

KING: It hurts to watch that, it really does...

YOUNG MAN: Sorry, sir.

KING: (*Looking him over.*) Well, you're not dressed like the average prince, I'll say that.

YOUNG MAN: No, sir...

KING: Not that it matters, of course--what's outside is less important than what's inside. (*Slight pause.*) What are you inside?

YOUNG MAN: Well...I'm afraid I'm not a prince, sir.

KING: (*Slight pause.*) You mean that, don't you.

YOUNG MAN: Yes, sir.

KING: (*A wry smile.*) A Young Man who admits he's not a prince--that's rare, to say the least. (*Pause.*) But you thought you'd try your luck anyway?

YOUNG MAN: Actually, sir, I-- (*Stops.*) No. I, er...I heard that Your Majesty's gardener might need a helper, and I thought perhaps...

KING: (*Chuckles.*) Say no more. A gardener! I should have known. You must think me very foolish, going on like that...

YOUNG MAN: No, sir! Not at all!

KING: Well, *I* think me very foolish, so I apologize. (*Rises from throne and starts out.*) The job is yours. Begin whenever you like, stay as long as it pleases you.

YOUNG MAN: Thank you, sir. (*The KING stops, as an idea strikes him.*) Is there...something else?

KING: (*Quieter, thinking.*) Hmmm...Your name, son?

YOUNG MAN: It's Michael, sir.

KING: Perhaps you could do something for me, Michael.

MICHAEL: If I can.

KING: (*Wandering down, as if to look out a window.*) My daughters...they love to walk in the garden in the afternoon. I watch them every day from the parapet. (*Thoughtfully.*) To see the...harshness of the world, spreading in all directions, and then this wall--and within it, such color, and life... They should have flowers. Every day. Would you do that for me?

MICHAEL: Of course. Shall I say they come from you?

KING: (*Slight pause.*) No. I would rather they enjoy them, not resent them. (*Starts out.*)

MICHAEL: Your Majesty...

KING: (*Stops.*) Yes?

MICHAEL: (*Hesitates, then.*) Any man would think himself blessed to have one beautiful daughter. You have twelve.

KING: (*Sighs.*) Twelve.

MICHAEL: And yet, you seem so filled with regret.

KING: Not regret. I regret nothing. But I cannot understand why they spite me so!

MICHAEL: Do they?

KING: Do they? (*Shakes his head; sits on the bench and motions for MICHAEL to sit next to him.*) I know you're just a gardener, but surely you've heard of this shoe situation.

MICHAEL: Vaguely.

KING: Well, there you are! Every day, the same simple question: "What do you do at night?" And every day the same answer: "Sleep, Father--what else?" And then they laugh--and the next morning, another pile of demolished shoes inside the door. And you ask if they spite me? (*Pause; easier.*) And the thing of it is...it wasn't always this way. When they were younger, we were so close. It seemed like there was always a child in my arms--sharing a secret, with a whisper, and a laugh. And when that child grew, there was another, and another, and another...And then suddenly it was done. No more. (*Slight pause; upstage, SHANNON crosses the stage, slowly and silently, reading a book. The KING watches her go by as he speaks*.) It's an odd feeling when you can no longer hold your child. When there *is* no child to hold--only a young...woman...who you do not seem to know, and who does not seem to want to know you. And the fact that you still love her--them--more than anything, seems to have become a wall, rather than a door. (*Pause*.) Something has happened to them that I can't know and they can't explain. So what can I do?

MICHAEL: What do you do?

KING: (*Rising to go*.) Lock them in, of course. I may not be able to hold them anymore, but I can keep them within arm's reach. They may not come to me anymore, but I can keep them from going too far.

MICHAEL: Due respect, sir, but...they seem to have found a way out.

KING: Well. We'll solve that problem--you can count on it. Good luck with your flowers, son. (*HE exits. Music filters in, as MICHAEL exits to the opposite side.*)

Scene 3

(*The Palace Gardens and Terrace--mid to late afternoon. The sound of the PRINCESSES approaching in clusters--chattering, giggling, etc. They are accompanied by a LADY-IN-WAITING, who carries a sewing basket--and who looks, wouldn't you know it, somewhat like the Music Teacher. SHE sits to the side and sews. And listens.)*

LUCY: ...All I'm saying is, you don't have to take it so seriously.

JESSI: (*Sniffs.*)   I happen to want to make a good impression.

HOLLY: Impression? You want their eyes to pop out of their heads.

SHANNON: (*Giggles.*) Holleeeeeee!

JESSI: (*Staring daggers at HOLLY.*) Oh, you should talk-- you don't care *who* you dance with--

LILY AND LINDSAY: (*Across the stage.*) Jessi! Sssssh!

JESSI: --as long as you get to lead...

LUCY: Look, nobody is criticizing you.

SHANNON: (*Brightly.*) Holly is!

LUCY: (*Glares at SHANNON, then:*) It's just that...we're just talking about men.

JESSI: Oh, is that all.

LUCY: Yes! And I think they just want to have fun, not...you know...get hypnotized or anything.

HOLLY: (*Pointing down to the ground.*) They're already hypnotized.

ASHLEY: (*A few feet away, listening; with a commanding tone of warning, even but not loud.*) Holly.

JESSI: (*A bit quieter.*) So, what? I'm supposed to be like Jill? (*JILL, across stage with NICOLE, perks up on hearing her name.*) Make myself look plainer than I am? Take the first boring prince that comes along?

SHANNON: (*At the top of her voice.*) JILLDIDYOU-JUSTHEARWHATJESSISAIDABOUTYOU?!!! (*Streaks over to JILL, who just looks glum, and begins whispering to her animatedly. HOLLY rolls her eyes.)*

JESSI: Or maybe I should be like Morgan-- (*MORGAN, in another group, doesn't flinch.*) Not care who I end up with because the world's going to burn up first?

MORGAN: It might.

LILY: It won't.

LINDSAY: It won't.

MORGAN: What if it does.

LUCY: (*To MORGAN.*) Then all you'll have are your memories. And I think those memories should be as wonderful and exciting and bright and beautiful as they can be. Not sad-- (*To JESSI.*) --and not fake and scheming and jealous. (*CHELSEA, in particular, listens intently.*)

NICOLE: (*Crosses to JESSI, near tears.*) I just want to say...that I think what you said about Jill was soooo terrible...

JILL: Nicole...

NICOLE: Because she has a heart, too, and she has dreams, too, and you never know. (*Gazing out and up, breathless.*) Someday the most beautiful, the most perfect prince might ride up searching for his heart's desire and see her there with the moonlight streaming through the trees and his heart will begin to race and music will come from nowhere and they'll run toward each other and he'll sweep her off her feet and onto his steed and they'll gallop off into the future where their two hearts will be as one forever and ever and ever and she'll just laugh. (*The PRINCESSES just stare at her.*)

HOLLY: (*After a slight pause.*) I know I will.

JILL: Listen, you know what you're doing? What we're all doing? We're all trying to figure out how to find The Right Prince.

LILY AND LINDSAY: Or Princes.

JILL: (*Slight smile.*) Or Princes. But the thing is, there's a Right One for each one of us--and we have to find him. Our own way.

ASHLEY: Haven't you all forgotten something?

JESSI: Such as?

ASHLEY: Such as...I can understand what you're all concerned about--that is, I can sort of understand--I mean, I'm going to be Queen someday, I can have anyone I want... But don't get so caught up in thinking about some foolish, everyday kind of man-- (*A wicked smile.*) --that you forget about perfection.

SARAH: Perfection?

ASHLEY: (*Indicating down.*) You know what I mean.

JILL: But we only see them at night.

ASHLEY: Wouldn't you rather have perfect romance some of the time than no romance all of the time?

NICOLE: Welllll...

SARAH: But they're still men, aren't they?

LUCY: So?

SARAH: So...I know what we want--I guess... But what do they want? (*Silence, as the PRINCESSES look at each other.*) I mean, we're kind of in this together...

ASHLEY: We're going to have trouble with you, aren't we.

SARAH: It's just a question. Someone must know the answer...

LADY-IN-WAITING: (*Still absorbed in her sewing.*) You could always ask your father.

ASHLEY: (*Slight pause; an imperious laugh.*) Pardon me?

LADY-IN-WAITING: He might tell you.

ASHLEY: In the first place, nobody asked your opinion.

SARAH: Ashley.

ASHLEY: In the second place, that is the last question we're likely to ask our father because it is the last question he is likely to answer.

LADY-IN-WAITING: Forgive me, my lady. I was merely trying to be helpful.

SHANNON: Maybe she does know.

JESSI: Don't be silly.

LILY: Why not?

LINDSAY: She's old enough...

ASHLEY: (*A mocking smile.*) Very well--if you insist. Tell us: what is it that men want.(*A few of the PRINCESSES chuckle.   During the following, MICHAEL wanders in. Dressed in a gardener's apron, with his bag around one shoulder, HE carries a basket filled with flower bouquets. The PRINCESSES do not see him.*)

LADY-IN-WAITING: The same thing that we want. (*A few of the PRINCESSES laugh outright.*) We want to choose and be chosen--they want to choose and be chosen. We want to love and be loved--they want to love and be loved. That's all.

HOLLY: Then why are they so...strange about it?

LADY-IN-WAITING: That, my dears, is the challenge. Trying to understand them is like trying to read your favorite book in a mirror. The story you love is right there--words and all. It's just...backwards. If it's any consolation, they think the same of us. The question is: (*Calmly turns toward MICHAEL, as though she knew he would be there.*) How to step through the mirror? (*The PRINCESSES follow her gaze, and there are sudden suppressed gasps and whispering. SARAH and MICHAEL spot each other.*)

ASHLEY: (*Stepping forward.*) Well, well, well. Speaking

of young men... We seem to be seeing quite a lot of this one, seem we not?

MICHAEL: (*A general bow of the head.*) M'lady.

ASHLEY: (*Circling him.*) And it appears that we will continue seeing you. (*The other PRINCESSES rush to join her.*) Garden boy, eh?

MICHAEL: Yes, please you.

ASHLEY: Please *me*? (*Laughs.*) I'm just one of twelve. I think you-- (*Pokes him.*) --need to worry about pleasing *all* of us. (*Pushes him into the crowd of PRINCESSES, from which only SARAH stands apart.*)

JILL: Where do you come from?

LILY AND LINDSAY: What brought you here?

LUCY: Do you have a name?

MICHAEL: It's Michael, m'lady. (*Scattered whispering and giggling.*)

ASHLEY: A common name. But then, you're a common young man, aren't you? (*Slight pause.*) What do the rest of you think? (*Scattered whispering and nudging, then:*)

SARAH: (*Quietly.*) I like him. Very much. (*THE REST erupt into laughs, whispers, squeals, sighs, etc.*)

SHANNON: Sarahhhhhh!

JESSI: (*Rolls her eyes.*) He's a gardener for gosh sakes...

HOLLY: At least remember who you are...

ASHLEY: (*Mocking.*) Now sisters, let's be fair. Maybe he has some special quality, beyond the dirt in his fingernails, that only Sarah can see. All right, "Michael". What pleasing thing have you done for us today?

MICHAEL: These flowers... I've brought them for you all. (*HE begins to hand out the bouquets, pausing just a moment with SARAH's.*)

HOLLY: (*A twinkle in her eye.*) Flowers?

LUCY: Really? (*SHANNON squeals slightly.*)

JILL: How lovely.

NICOLE: That is sooo romantic...

MORGAN: They're probably dead.

MICHAEL: No, m'lady. They're as beautiful as the Princesses who carry them. (*In spite of themselves, the PRINCESSES begin to be charmed. Except for:*)

ASHLEY: You're obviously a very clever young man. I suppose we can tolerate you a while longer. (*A tower bell begins to toll five. The LADY-IN-WAITING packs up her sewing and stands by the exit.*) Just know your place and keep to it, and we'll get along fine. (*The PRINCESSES begin to drift off, smelling their bouquets and whispering among themselves.*)

MICHAEL: Yes, m'lady. (*Hands ASHLEY the last bouquet; she smells it, looks at him with a tight smile, then pulls him aside.*)

ASHLEY: Oh--and if you should happen to think about intruding in any, how shall I say, private business of ours...don't. It wouldn't be healthy. (*SHE wheels and glides off. SARAH starts to follow, but turns back.*)

SARAH: Michael...

MICHAEL: My lady...

SARAH: (*Pause.*) These are lovely. Thank you. (*MICHAEL nods, without taking his eyes off her.*) Tomorrow?

MICHAEL: (*Smiles.*) Tomorrow. (*A moment; SARAH smiles back, then runs off. A pause, and HE reaches into his bag and pulls out the magic cloak.*) No. Tonight. (*Turns and runs off. Music up as the scene changes.*)

*

Scene 4

*(The Princesses' Bedchamber—later that evening. None
of the furniture need actually be visible; more important
is the appearance of the PRINCESSES themselves.
They now wear long, high-collared nightshirts or robes
over their dresses—and shoes—and each carries a
pillow. As they rush in excitedly, in groups of three or
four, a pillow fight breaks out. ASHLEY is the last to
enter; the fight stops at her warning glance—then erupts
again with even more glee than before. A moment, and
a handbell is heard. A CHAMBERMAID enters,
ringing it, trying to get the girls to settle down. The
CHAMBERMAID, as you might imagine, bears a more
than passing resemblance to the Lady-In-Waiting...*

*Suddenly, the KING is standing there, holding a heavy
key chain—which contains three extremely large and
severe looking keys. These are not dainty, fairyland
keys: these clearly fit a set of locks that mean business.
As soon as HE enters, the bedtime chatter quiets down,
and the PRINCESSES form up across the stage, pillows
held in front of them.)*

ASHLEY: *(With extreme politeness.)*   Good evening,
Father.

THE OTHER PRINCESSES: *(Excepting of course,*

CHELSEA.) Good evening, Father.

KING: (*Equally polite, but also with an edge.*) Well, we'll see--won't we? (*Wanders slowly past his daughters.*) Bathed...powdered...dressed...

CHAMBERMAID: Yes, your Majesty.

KING: Hair brushed...Pillows fluffed...Windows *locked*... All ready for a good night's sleep, hmmm? (*SHANNON giggles, then stops abruptly.*) Oh, yes. And all those lovely shoes. Just waiting.

HOLLY: (*Wryly.*) All alone, Father?

KING: For a change.

LUCY: No prince outside the door tonight?

KING: (*His blood pressure rising a bit.*) A fat lot it matters to you.

JESSI: I don't know, that last one was pretty cute...

KING: You thought so? WELL NOW HE'S PRETTY DEAD! AND IT'S ALL BECAUSE YOU-- (*Stops, choking on his words, then controls himself. To the Chambermaid.*) You may go. (*The CHAMBERMAID curtseys and exits. A pause.*) How long is this going to go on. (*ASHLEY starts to speak.*) And don't say "What". Because we all know "What". In fact, I've almost decided to stop asking about the "What"-- because I despair of ever having an answer! (*Behind him, MICHAEL steps in--wearing the magic cloak.*) But I would like to know-- (*Stops, sensing something that he can't define, and looks around.*)

JILL: Like to know what, Father?

KING: Hmmmm. (*Shakes it off.*) I would like to know "Why". (*Pause; looking at each one.*) Lucy? (*SHE shrugs.*) Jill? (*SHE purses her lips.*) Lil-- Linds-- Ughh... (*THEY look at each other, then back at him.*) Holly? (*A wry smile crosses her face.*) Morgan. (*SHE sighs an existential sigh.*)

Shannon? (*SHE bites her lip.*) Nicole? (*Holding back tears, SHE buries her head in her pillow.*) Jessi. (*SHE tosses her head, and preens some more.*) Chelsea… (*SHE starts to say something, then looks at ASHLEY and looks down.*) Ashley. (*SHE looks at him defiantly; HE looks back hard at her, pointing the keys in his fist. Then, a bit quieter:*) Sarah… (*SHE looks up at him, then down, somewhat sadly. A pause.*) As you wish. (*Looks at them all once more; with heavy irony.*) Sleep well. (*HE exits. Complete stillness. Then, the sound of an immensely heavy door creaking shut and slamming. The PRINCESSES look at each other and start to smile. Then we hear the sound of three enormous bolts being thrown and padlocked. MICHAEL stands, motionless, as the last bolt is thrown and the sound of the lock echoes unnaturally in the distance. Instantly, the orderly line of PRINCESSES dissolves in a rush of excited activity…*)

*

Interlude

(*As ethereal music filters in, MICHAEL begins to describe the action which happens around him. His speeches, out of time, may be spoken live, or on a voice-over at first, eventually blending into live performance as the Interlude progresses.*)

MICHAEL: How can I begin to tell what I saw, during the course of that night, as I watched--invisible to all eyes... The moment the door was closed and locked, and the King's footsteps had receded down the darkened hallway, the bedroom suddenly filled with laughter. (*It does. The PRINCESSES help each other to remove their nightgowns; a few carry the gowns offstage and return with garlands for their hair, garlands which match the dresses.*) Each Princess transformed before my eyes--each Princess lovelier than the one who came before her. Faces were made up and headdresses put in place so quickly you would think night was nearly over and not just begun. Once or twice I felt sure that I had been seen, so clearly did I feel a pair of eyes looking through me. But I soon realized that all was as the old woman promised. I could indeed follow them anywhere--and they would never know... (*The change is complete. The PRINCESSES gather around the downstage bench.*)[*See Scenic Notes following script.*] Suddenly, without a word, the Princesses gathered--and clapped their hands. (*THEY do so, three times. Two of them grasp the bench top-- which they open slowly.*) To my astonishment, what seemed to be solid stone opened easily--and light from another world, beyond this time and place, streamed into the room. (*Bright, unreal light shines up and out, as the PRINCESSES--shielding themselves from it, but drawn to it--move toward the bench. One PRINCESS helps a second to begin to step inside.*) And with that they stepped, one by one, through the opening. (*Blackout. In the dark, the PRINCESSES make their escape.*) I was so entranced that I almost forgot to follow--but I managed to slip through before it sealed up behind me. (*The ethereal music continues, as light slowly begins to fill the space. A different kind of light, the light of the forest. MICHAEL moves through it, wondering at what he sees.*) I found myself on a path that wound through the thickest forest I had ever seen. But it was not an earthly forest--for the leaves that hung from the branches were made of gold and silver, and the buds that grew between them were diamonds--every one... We continued through the wood--until, presently, lights could be seen through the trees. And just as suddenly as we were in the wood, we were out of it--on the shore of a huge lake. Beyond which, on an island, rose a castle--lights shining in the darkness, music pouring out of it. (*Faint dance music is heard in the distance.*) As we approached the shore, twelve boats appeared on the lake--each rowed by a prince--who said nothing, but helped each Princess on board. I stepped carefully onto the last boat--and soon we reached the island, and the castle. (*The lights begin to blaze in the direction of the castle, and the music is louder. THE PRINCESSES enter--ASHLEY first, SARAH last.*) The Princesses chattered away as though it were nothing unusual, but I was so absorbed by the sight around me that, quite by accident... (*HE steps accidentally on the train of SARAH's dress.*)

SARAH: Oh! (*The parade stops suddenly--and so does the music.*)

JILL: Sarah?

NICOLE: What is it?

SARAH: (*Looking around.*) I don't know. For a moment I thought-- (*Stops.*)

ASHLEY: (*Frowning, wary.*) Thought what?

SARAH: That someone stepped on my dress.

LUCY: (*Laughs.*) You're kidding.

SHANNON: But there's nobody there.

HOLLY: Woooooo--spooky... (*Chuckles.*)

LILY AND LINDSAY: Maybe it was a ghost!

MORGAN: (*Darkly.*) Maybe it was your fate.

JESSI: Maybe it was your gardener. (*General laughter--
except for SARAH, who looks right at MICHAEL but doesn't
see him. A pause.*)
SARAH: I must have caught it on a nail. It's nothing.
ASHLEY: (*Frowns, looking at SARAH; then smiles,
grandly.*) Sisters, the evening awaits. (*The music starts again,
and the PRINCESSES move on. The stage now becomes the
enchanted castle, and the PRINCESSES begin to dance. In a
group at first, then with solos weaving through the group; some
may disappear to other parts of the "castle", where we might
catch occasional glimpses of them dancing with ghostly
partners.*)
MICHAEL: (*Wandering through, unobserved.*) And so
they went, and so I followed. I saw room after room, reaching
off almost forever, where orchestras played, and banquets were
laid out, and the Princesses danced and danced with a dozen
enchanted princes. I stood under the blazing chandeliers and
watched them--each dancing in her own way, yet each in the
thrall of the secret. Of the magic. (*SARAH moves away from
the group--still dancing, but alone, with a thoughtful look on
her face. MICHAEL follows her from a distance.*) Except for
the Princess Sarah. Oh, she danced--gracefully, easily--but
something was missing. Her mind seemed to be on something
else... Almost as though she wished she were elsewhere. Or,
perhaps, that she were dancing with someone who was not
there. (*SARAH is dancing by herself--arms out, holding an
imaginary partner. MICHAEL watches--or, perhaps, begins to
partner her, at a slight remove, matching her move for move.
At length, LUCY and HOLLY walk into the room, fanning
themselves from the evening's exertions.*)
LUCY: Whew...It's a great night tonight, isn't it?
HOLLY: I should hope so. (*Stops as they see SARAH.*)

Well, well, well.

  LUCY: (*Laughs.*) What have we here? (*SARAH stops suddenly.*)

  HOLLY: No, no, don't stop...

  LUCY: Please!

  HOLLY: May I cut in? (*SHE and LUCY laugh.*)

  SARAH: (*Embarrassed.*) I'm finished.

  LUCY: Come on, Sarah, don't take it so seriously...

  SARAH: Leave me alone. (*LUCY and HOLLY look at each other; LUCY laughs slightly and HOLLY shakes her head. JESSI and MORGAN and NICOLE appear.*)

  NICOLE: This is just the best... I think I'm in love.

  JESSI: You always think you're in love.

  NICOLE: No, but tonight...it's just so utterly perfect in every way... Perfect music, perfect princes...(*SHE begins dancing by herself to the music.*)

  MORGAN: And it all ends at dawn. How depressing.

  JESSI: Oh, will you stop? Honestly...I hope you choke.

  MORGAN: Wouldn't surprise me. Nothing would surprise me. (*LILY and LINDSAY enter.*)

  LUCY: Oh no? How about, our little sister doesn't think any of our partners are good enough.

  LILY AND LINDSAY: Really?! (*They giggle.*)

  SARAH: That's enough.

  JESSI: Sarah, what has gotten into you?

  SARAH: Nothing has "gotten into me". I just--

  HOLLY: If you ask me, I think she's the one who's in love.

  LILY AND LINDSAY: In love?!

  MORGAN: Not another one. (*JILL enters, followed by ASHLEY.*)

  LUCY: (*Looking off toward the rest of the castle.*) So

which one is he?

JESSI: (*A bit jealous*.) Yes--which one.

JILL: Which one what?

NICOLE: (*Goes to SARAH and hugs her.*) I'm soooo happy for you...

MICHAEL: This is intolerable!

SHANNON: (*Streaking in.*) What'd I miss? What'd I miss?

LUCY: Little sister is in love with...somebody.

ASHLEY: What?

LILY AND LINDSAY: There's always somebody...

HOLLY: Even if you only imagine them.

SARAH: All right. It *was* my imagination. I was dreaming to myself. Are you satisfied?

ASHLEY: (*From across the room, taking command.*) No. (*And the music abruptly stops.*) I am not satisfied. (*Pause; moves to SARAH.*) I would be very careful if I were you.

SARAH: (*Almost instinctively rising to challenge her.*) Careful of what.

ASHLEY: Careful not to forget who you are.

SARAH: (*A flash of pride and defiance in her voice.*) I am a Princess--the daughter of a king. Just as you are.

ASHLEY: Exactly. As we all are. (*Pointedly, as much to the others as to SARAH.*) Dreaming otherwise is foolish. And dangerous.

SARAH: But I have to be myself.

ASHLEY: Within limits.

LUCY: (*To HOLLY.*) Now she sounds like Father.

ASHLEY: (*Turning on her.*) No. Father cares only about himself. I care about us. Don't forget, *I* was first to know the secret of this place. And I passed it on, in turn, to each of you--did I not? (*Silence.*) It was my gift to you all--a secret knowledge that would bind us together in a way that nothing could break. No matter what happens to any of us, in this thing, we would be sisters--forever. I asked nothing in return-- except your silence. Which you swore to. (*Directly at SARAH.*) Every one of you.

SARAH: I have said nothing.

ASHLEY: I see that look on your face--don't think I don't. I fear that it no longer wants my gift. I fear...that it wants to speak for one, instead of twelve.

SARAH: (*Drawing herself up.*) What if I did.

ASHLEY: In the cause of worldly love? (*Chuckles and shakes her head.*)

SARAH: You don't believe in it, do you.

ASHLEY: (*Slight pause; quietly intense.*) It dies, Sarah. It holds you in its arms, and smiles down at you, and makes you the center of its world until you can't remember when it wasn't there--and then it dies. And when you look around for something to ease the pain of this...desertion...you see only stone faces, that turn away from you--as though you were foolish to be so trusting. As though you should have known better. (*Simply.*) So. I know better. Nothing dies, here. (*Moves away, turns and smiles, and gestures.*) Dance, my sisters, and be happy. This, at least, we can call our own. (*The music begins again--slower this time. The other PRINCESSES exit quietly, whispering among themselves, except for ASHLEY and SARAH, who stand apart, looking at each other. And CHELSEA, who looks at both for a moment, then dances off between them--slowly, elegantly, reflectively. The lights have altered--and ASHLEY and SARAH begin their own brief dance: almost a pas-de-deux, mirroring each other at first, eye to eye, equally regal, but with a new understanding of each other. ASHLEY eventually takes center stage, her dancing an expression of her strength and confidence—as SARAH circles her slowly, her own pride muted, her heart and spirit wanting to break through, but unable to. Throughout, MICHAEL remains at the side, watching.)*

MICHAEL: (*After the dance has begun.*) And they did dance--until the first light of dawn, when the music stopped, and the lights of the castle were dimmed, and the boats ferried them back across the lake. (*ASHLEY and SARAH continue their dance for a moment, and then move off through separate exits, with a last look at each other.*) They made their way back through the forest, and again I followed. This time, as we passed beneath the trees, I took for myself the proof I knew I would need: (*HE gathers them from the unseen trees—or perhaps they fall gently to the stage, gleaming in the light.*) A leaf of gold, and a leaf of silver, and a diamond bud. If I gave them to the King the next morning, when the door was opened, and told him the secret of the shoes, the choice would be mine to make. But what if she did not want to be chosen? I had to know. (*The lights begin to fade up from magical light into the real light of day. MICHAEL removes the cloak, and places it and the leaves into his travelling bag which is now at the side of the stage.*) As I crept, unseen, from the Princesses' room-- past the tattered shoes, past the King who stared at them with a weary sigh--I thought I knew how to find out... (*HE sets the bag aside, retrieves some gardening tools, and begins the day's work--now in the castle garden.*)

*

Scene 5

(The Castle Garden—late the following morning. MICHAEL is working. A moment, and a SERVANT crosses the stage, carrying a large silver tray. On it are a mound of tattered shoes. The SERVANT is muttering to himself, ad-lib, as he passes; every day it's the same thing—and they certainly can't smell very good... MICHAEL watches him go, and smiles to himself.

A moment, and SARAH runs on from the opposite side of the stage. SHE wears new shoes, and in her hand carries the day's flower bouquet. She glances quickly behind her; then SHE removes a gold leaf from the bouquet, looks at it, and conceals it. She looks at MICHAEL, and approaches with as much control as she can manage.)

SARAH: Michael. (*MICHAEL turns, and starts to kneel.*)
MICHAEL: My lady, I-- (*SHE holds out a hand to stop him.*)
SARAH: Please. Say nothing. (*SHE walks toward him slowly, and holds out the bouquet.*) Where did you get these.
MICHAEL: (*Slight pause.*) From the garden, of course...
SARAH: I don't mean the flowers. (*Holds out the gold leaf.*) You know.
MICHAEL: (*Slight pause.*) Yes.
SARAH: But how?
MICHAEL: I followed you.
SARAH: That's impossible. I never saw you.

MICHAEL: I was...hidden, my lady.

SARAH: And so you saw everything.

MICHAEL: Yes.

SARAH: And heard... (*MICHAEL says nothing, merely looks at her. SHE considers this, then:*) You know what my father is offering for this secret. (*MICHAEL nods.*) Do you plan to tell him?

MICHAEL: Should I?

SARAH: I asked whether you would.

MICHAEL: (*Slight pause.*) Why do you keep it from him?

SARAH: You heard Ashley.

MICHAEL: I'm not talking about Ashley. I'm talking about you.

SARAH: (*Puts on an air of haughtiness.*) My father locks us in, after all. If we find a way out, why should we tell him and ruin it?

MICHAEL: He says he does it because he loves you.

SARAH: That makes no sense. I refuse to believe it.

MICHAEL: There are many unbelievable things done for the sake of love.

SARAH: (*A bit of a challenge.*) Such as?

MICHAEL: Such as...young men who risk their heads for the hand of a princess.

SARAH: Do they do that for love?

MICHAEL: They must.

SARAH: (*Shakes her head.*) I've seen them. They want the trappings. They want a crown, a castle, the fortune that goes with it. They love what a princess stands for--not who she really is. (*The false haughtiness slips; genuinely hopeful:*) What about you? Are you a fortune-hunter too?

MICHAEL: (*Slight pause.*) If I loved someone--enough

to risk everything...the trappings wouldn't matter.

SARAH: Wouldn't they?

MICHAEL: If my own did not matter to her.

SARAH: (*Pause; quietly.*) We don't even know each other.

MICHAEL: I think we do.

SARAH: (*Wanting to believe.*) If I could be sure...

MICHAEL: (*Kneels suddenly.*) Test me.

SARAH: (*Looking around, fearful of being caught.*) Please...

MICHAEL: Ask anything of me--I will do it.

SARAH: Someone might see us!

MICHAEL: Give me a challenge.

SARAH: Michael... (*Thinks a moment, then:*) The secret.

MICHAEL: Yes?

SARAH: Of the shoes. The secret that would reward you if you revealed it...

MICHAEL: That would allow me to make my choice.

SARAH: (*Slight pause, quietly.*) Keep it secret. (*Pause.*) For now. (*They look at each other intensely for a moment, then:*)

MICHAEL: (*Simply.*) As you wish. (*Pause; SHE holds out her hand to help him rise--but he takes it, and kisses it gently. A moment; she smiles, and he smiles back. Then MICHAEL walks off. SARAH looks after him, then exits in another direction. A slight pause--and from behind the scenery, ASHLEY enters, her face angry and set. She is accompanied by CHELSEA and JESSI.*)

ASHLEY: How dare she.

JESSI: I told you something was wrong with her.

ASHLEY: After all I've done for her...to let that--that *boy* think that he has some chance with her...

JESSI: How could he have hidden himself?   We saw everything!

ASHLEY: I don't know. But I'll tell you this. We must stop this at once. (*CHELSEA starts to speak.*) The question is, how?

JESSI: We could go to Father.

ASHLEY: Don't be ridiculous.

JESSI: Why not? There are dungeons for a reason.

ASHLEY: Because the first thing he would do is tell Father the secret--and that is exactly what I'm trying to avoid. (*Thinks a second--then smiles a very sly smile.*) Yes. I agree with Sarah. (*CHELSEA brightens.*)

JESSI: You *do*?

ASHLEY: Of course. As long as he knows, there's no point continuing this little game of hide and seek.   So I think...it's high time we made him welcome.

JESSI: You've got to be kidding.

ASHLEY: Not at all. If he wants to visit our little party so badly, I think it would be bad manners not to invite him.

JESSI: Ashley!

ASHLEY: I think he'll enjoy meeting the rest of our young men. So much so--that I don't think he'll ever want to leave. So he won't. (*CHELSEA is suddenly wide-eyed.*)

JESSI: (*Catches her breath.*) You're serious.

ASHLEY: (*Deadly serious.*) Sarah wants him so badly? She can have him, every night--for eternity.

JESSI: But how will you do it?

ASHLEY: The same as with the others. A frozen heart is easily obtained--if one knows the right potion to administer. (*Slight pause.*) But I'll take care of that. Jessi, see if you can find him a particularly sumptuous set of clothes--after all, one should be dressed properly for a dance. (*JESSI smiles conspiratorially.)* And Chelsea... (*CHELSEA, who was starting to slip away, turns with a start.*) An invitation. Something to entice him to join us--he can conceal himself in our room before we get there. (*Pointedly.*) I'll speak to little sister. (*Then, looking off toward where MICHAEL exited.*) You want a challenge, garden boy? We'll give you a challenge... (*And she sweeps out, followed by JESSI and a very hesitant CHELSEA. A moment--and the LADY-IN-WAITING steals in. SHE scans the stage furtively, looking for something, until she finds it: MICHAEL's bag. SHE pulls out the magic cloak.*)

LADY-IN-WAITING: (*Quietly.*) Trust who you are, Michael--and what you know... (*SHE picks up the cloak and the bag and moves off, as the lights fade quickly.*)

*

Scene 6

(*In the darkness the sound of the three giant locks being locked is amplified and echoes in the space. From out of it comes the sound of the dance music--faint at first, then louder. The magical lights fade up; we are once again in the underground castle.*

The dancing is in progress; it seems somehow even brighter and livelier, because this time it is for Michael's benefit. SARAH, in particular, looks radiant. MICHAEL--who wears a stunning suit of expensive clothes--dances with her for a while, but begins to find himself spirited away by the other PRINCESSES, who are swirling around him, vying for his attention.   At length the dance ends in laughter and some applause; the group breaks up, with MICHAEL and SARAH arm in arm--and ASHLEY watching and waiting.)

NICOLE: *(Gushing.)* This is just the most wonderful night we have ever had...

LUCY: You say that every night. *(To MICHAEL.)* She says that every night.

NICOLE: Oh, but this night... *(Beaming at MICHAEL and SARAH.)* I don't think it could ever be as special as this.

MICHAEL: I'm honored that you've allowed me to come here, to share this with you. *(SARAH smiles up at him.)* And the clothes--you certainly thought of everything.

JESSI: *(Deadly.)* I chose them myself.

MICHAEL: *(Just a hair nervous.)* Well. I appreciate your making me feel so welcome.

ASHLEY: *(From across the room--a bit too charming.)* How could we not? Once we knew that you had learned our secret, it would have been silly not to make you a part of it.

SHANNON: Sarah didn't think you should come with us.

SARAH: *(Embarrassed.)* Shannon...

SHANNON: It's true... *(MICHAEL looks at SARAH a bit quizzically.)*

ASHLEY: *(Quickly.)* I think...she was afraid she might lose you. *(SARAH frowns; CHELSEA looks worried.)* And who can blame her? Now that you know the rest of us, who knows what you might decide? *(Laughter and chatter from the rest.)* But not to worry. We love her dearly--and what makes her happy, makes us happy.

SARAH: (*A bit suspicious, but willing to give her the benefit of the doubt.*) Thank you, Ashley.

MICHAEL: I promise you, all. Her happiness is a trust. I will not betray it. (*To SARAH.*) And you will not lose me.

LUCY: I should have known. You meet a prince--he usually turns out to be dirt. You meet someone who works in the dirt--he turns out to be a prince... (*Across the room, ASHLEY nods to JESSI, who sidles over to MICHAEL.*)

JESSI: Well *I* wish that some of us could get to know this "prince" better.

NICOLE: Oh, yesssssssss...

SHANNON: Could we dance with him? Huh, Sarah? Could we? Just one dance, Sarah? Huh? Just one?

LUCY: (*Genially.*) Sure--you've had him all evening, how about giving some of the rest of us a turn?

JESSI: It won't mean anything--honest it won't.

ASHLEY: Why not? One dance--and then some refreshment for our guest. (*A clamor of assent.*)

MICHAEL: (*To SARAH.*) Do you mind?

SARAH: (*Smiles.*) Just one. (*MICHAEL gives her hand a quick kiss. SHE puts on a slightly regal air, a twinkle in her eye.*) One moment. I must know for whom you would leave me.

MICHAEL: (*Looking around.*) I don't know. What do you think? (*SARAH whispers something to him, and he nods.*) I would consider that a pleasure. (*Looks down the row of waiting PRINCESSES--beyond them, to the one who stands apart.*) Jill? May I?

JILL: (*Smiles, shyly.*) Of course. (*MICHAEL takes her arm, and they stroll off to another part of the castle to dance. A slight pause, and the others follow in a rush to watch. JESSI and ASHLEY exit last of all, exchanging sly grins. SARAH is left downstage; she watches the others go, and sighs audibly— but for the first time it is a sigh of happiness. A moment—and her reverie is broken by a voice.)*

CHELSEA: *(Whispering.)* Sarah! *(SARAH turns slightly, not certain of what she hears.)* Sarah!

SARAH: *(Now turns to see her; in mild disbelief.)* Chelsea?

CHELSEA: Sssssh! There's not much time--

SARAH: Chelsea, what are you--?

CHELSEA: Please--just listen! There's something you must know.

SARAH: What's the matter?

CHELSEA: It's Michael. There is danger for him here.

SARAH: Danger?!

CHELSEA: Sssssh!

SARAH: How is there danger?

CHELSEA: Ashley. This welcome is a lie--she's furious that he knows the secret.

SARAH: But he's sworn to keep silent. He promised me!

CHELSEA: Sarah, she doesn't even trust you. She's certainly not going to trust him. *(Slight pause.)* She will offer him a drink tonight, that will freeze his heart in enchantment and bind him to this place forever. There will be no escape for him if he takes it.

SARAH: No! *(SHE starts to run off, but CHELSEA stops her.)*

CHELSEA: Sarah--

SARAH: Please--help me...

CHELSEA: Listen! *(SARAH stops.)* It's not as simple as you think. Believe me, it's not.

SARAH: *(Slight pause.)* How long have you known?

CHELSEA: Since this afternoon.

SARAH: And you didn't try to stop her?!

CHELSEA: I can't stop her. I've never been able to--you know that.

SARAH: Then why have you told me this?

CHELSEA: Because I can't let her decide for you. She has decided too much for us already. This choice, at least, should be yours.

SARAH: I've already made it. (*Starts out.*)

CHELSEA: Sarah, wait... (*SARAH stops again, impatiently.*) This castle--that we come to, every night...you know how much it means to us.

SARAH: Of course I do.

CHELSEA: Then you must understand. To save him will be to destroy this place.

SARAH: (*Slight pause.*) I would never do that.

CHELSEA: The secret will be known, and the spell will be broken--it must be.

SARAH: But I can't decide that for you.

CHELSEA: Then you will have to let him go. (*Slight pause.*) There is no other way it can be. And Ashley knows it. (*Pause; SARAH looks off toward the dancing.*)

SARAH: Why is she so determined to control me?

CHELSEA: Because she needs you--desperately. Don't you see? She looks at you, and she sees the person who took our mother away from us. If you had never been born...

SARAH: (*Stricken.*) Chelsea...

CHELSEA: I'm telling you how she sees you! (*Slight pause.*) She never grieved, Sarah. As long as you're here, she doesn't have to--she can be angry, and defiant, and alone, and blame you for it. And the worst thing is, for all their anger toward each other, she and Father are exactly the same. They want to keep life from hurting--and they just end up making it...I don't know. Hollow. (*Pause.*) I wish I knew how to bring us all closer together. Maybe... the best we can hope for is not to grow any farther apart.

SARAH: (*Quietly.*) What should I do?

CHELSEA: (*The truth.*) I don't know. I'm not sure I could tell you--even if I did know. (*Slight pause.*) Perhaps Ashley's right.

SARAH: Surely you don't believe that.

CHELSEA: (*Considers.*) Well, after all...this we do have. This we do know. Everything else--the future...we don't have it, and we don't know it. At least you'd always have Michael, here. (*SARAH thinks about this.*) I'm sorry. I just...I thought you should know. (*Pause, as they look at each other, CHELSEA somewhat sadly. The music ends, and there is applause and then chatter and giggling from the other room. MICHAEL enters, with JILL on one arm; she eventually moves off as the other PRINCESSES crowd into the room— except JESSI, who does not enter. The chatter and whispering and giggling continue, until ASHLEY steps forward and takes charge.*)

MICHAEL: (*A slight bow to JILL.*) And thank you again for the dance.

JILL: (*As glowing as we've yet seen her.*) You're welcome. (*SHE moves off, smiling at SARAH as she passes— but SARAH does not smile back. She's staring at MICHAEL.*)

SHANNON: Sarahhhhh! You missed it!

SARAH: Did I.

SHANNON: They looked soooooo great together!

LUCY: Shannon!

SHANNON: Well, I mean, not *together* together, but... oh, you know... (*During the following, MICHAEL begins to sense that there's something wrong, and takes a step toward*

SARAH—who says nothing.)
  NICOLE: I would never let him go…
  HOLLY: And he didn't step on her feet once. I'd marry him for *that.*
  ASHLEY: (*Stepping forward, with a chiding laugh.*) Now, now, let's not frighten the poor young man with talk of marriage. (*SHE takes MICHAEL's arm, distracting him from SARAH.*) I think it's quite enough to enjoy ourselves without thinking of the future. (*A "sudden thought".*) Oh--I almost forgot! I promised you some refreshment, didn't I?
  MICHAEL: (*Smiles.*) I wouldn't mind a little something, if you have it.
  ASHLEY: Anything for you--right, sisters? (*At that moment, JESSI appears, holding a silver chalice.*) And here we are. (*SARAH watches as JESSI walks over with the cup—then SARAH turns away, unable or unwilling to say anything.*)
  JESSI: (*Looking him square in the eye as she holds out the chalice.*) We'll dance another time.
  MICHAEL: Yes. Another time. (*Takes the cup, and raises it in a toast to the PRINCESSES.*) To the first of many visits. (*HE starts to drink, then turns once more.*) And…to Sarah. (*HE raises the cup as SARAH turns to look at him. HE starts to drink--and then… Everyone freezes, as a sudden, dramatic shift of lights occurs. Figures are lit partially or completely, from many angles and in many intensities. At the same time, music which is more distorted than melodic invades the scene—along with a very low rumbling not unlike a far-off earthquake. MICHAEL lowers the cup and looks around. As he does, ASHLEY takes stage--defiantly, advancing on MICHAEL. HE looks to SARAH, but ASHLEY has blocked him. SHE makes a bold gesture in his direction, and he is instantly surrounded by a group of PRINCESSES. THEY circle*

him slowly, ritualistically, as though controlled by ASHLEY—literally weaving a spell around him. SARAH makes a sudden move toward them; her movement, like the others, is more balletic. Then she looks to a second group of PRINCESSES, and then to a third, appealing to her sisters for help. Each group turns away at a gesture from ASHLEY. SARAH realizes that it's up to her—and she moves quickly to step between ASHLEY and MICHAEL, staring ASHLEY down. SARAH makes a bold gesture of her own, and the first group of PRINCESSES stop circling MICHAEL. SARAH breaks the circle, scattering the PRINCESSES; those who turned away now turn in to watch. SARAH suddenly grabs the chalice away from MICHAEL, and turns to ASHLEY. ASHLEY steps toward SARAH threateningly, but is stopped when SARAH raises the chalice. A pause—and she throws the contents across the floor. [If the potion is not in fact imaginary, then use of glitter might be effective.] Then SARAH tosses the chalice to ASHLEY, reaches back, and takes MICHAEL's hand. THEY start out—but before they can leave, the quiet rumbling sound begins to get louder. And louder. Everyone stands transfixed, looking up and around. The lights begin to flare and go out; SARAH and MICHAEL run out quickly. The other PRINCESSES begin to scatter in different directions—perhaps with a scream or a cry—as the stage darkens. ASHLEY remains unmoving—chalice in her hand, defeated, watching as her dream crumbles around her. Finally she is alone on stage, the sound of chaos at its height—as CHELSEA moves quickly back in and takes her by the hand. A brief tug, an unwilling response—and then THE TWO exit together. The stage is dark.)

*

Scene 7

*(The Princesses' Bedchamber.   Early morning light
filtering into the room. MICHAEL and SARAH run on,
almost out of breath. A pause; as they try to catch their
breath, they stand, holding hands—but not looking at
each other. Then:)*

SARAH: Safe?

MICHAEL: *(Pause; HE nods.)* Safe. *(Another breathless
pause, which becomes a shared sigh of exhaustion and relief.
Silence—still holding hands, still not daring to look at each
other. And then, very quietly:)* I love you.

SARAH: *(Pause; SHE turns to look at him. Equally
quietly:)* I love you. *(Slight pause.)* And...I choose you. No
matter what may become of us.

MICHAEL: *(Turning to look at her.)* And I, you.
Because of what may become of us.*(A pause. THEY kiss,
and/or embrace each other—and are immediately interrupted by
a flood of PRINCESSES who stream into the room, having fled
the crumbling castle.)*

LUCY: *(Entering.)* I can't believe it--I just can't believe
it... *(Stops short as she sees MICHAEL and SARAH.)*

SHANNON: *(Running on.)* Ohmygoshl'veneverrunsofastin
mylifeIthoughtwe'dnevermakeit...

HOLLY: *(Strolling on behind SHANNON.)* Amazing how
fast those guys can row when they put their minds to it...

LILY: *(By herself–frantic.)* Lindsay? Where are you?!
LINDSAY?!

JILL: *(Drifting in, very sad.)* That beautiful forest--the
gold and the silver trees, they were falling everywhere...

LILY: LINDSAY?!!

LINDSAY: *(Running on from the opposite side.)* Lily?!
Where are you?! *(LILY and LINDSAY see each other and fall

into each others' arms.)

MORGAN: (*Walking slowly in, with NICOLE and JESSI.*) Well, that's the end of that.

NICOLE: (*Distraught.*) It was soooooooooo awful...

MORGAN: (*Brooding.*) Towers on fire, walls collapsing into the lake, enchanted princes swallowed up by the earth... (*Suddenly smiles—for the first time.*) It was great.

JESSI: (*In disbelief.*) It's all gone, isn't it? We can never go back there again...(*To SARAH, bitterly:*) I hope you're happy.

SARAH: Where's Ashley?

JESSI: As if you care.

SARAH: I do. Where is she?

ASHLEY: (*Enters slowly; she holds the empty chalice.*) I'm here. (*SHE moves slowly toward SARAH, as though her rage might flare up again, then stops.*) I only want to know one thing... (*Looking around at the other Princesses.*) Who told her? (*A slight pause; then:*)

CHELSEA: (*Who has entered behind.*) Who knows? (*ASHLEY stares at CHELSEA, mouth agape. Before she can say anything, we hear the sound of the three massive locks being unlocked.*)

LILY AND LINDSAY: It's Father!

NICOLE: What shall we do?

SHANNON: What shall we say?

ASHLEY: Nothing. Absolutely nothing. Let me do the talking. (*To them all, desperately.*) We can have it back. We can make it come back! (*SHE hides the chalice behind her back, as THE KING enters—already weary. He is accompanied by the SERVANT who carries the large silver tray; it is, of course, empty.*)

KING: Good morning, good morning, good morning. But

enough pleasantries. I've an extremely busy day ahead, so let us get to the point, shall we? For the last time, I demand to know. How did these shoes come to be torn to pieces during the night?! (*Looks at the tray. A pause.*) One moment. (*Looks around; no shoes anywhere.*) All right. What happened to the shoes.

MICHAEL: I think I can explain, sire.

KING: (*Looking at the PRINCESSES.*) Just a minute, Michael, please. What are you all dressed like this for? What do you all look so morose for? (*Slight pause.*) And for heaven's sake, what's he doing in here?

MICHAEL: I have the answer you seek, Your Majesty. I have learned the secret of the shoes. (*Muffled reactions from the other PRINCESSES.*)

KING: What's that?!

ASHLEY: It's a lie!

SARAH: If you would just listen, Father--

ASHLEY: He's a scoundrel and a thief--you can't believe a word he says!

KING: Considering that I can't believe a word *you've* said up to now, I will take my chances. (*To MICHAEL.*) All right, son. Let's have it.

MICHAEL: (*Circling the room, the PRINCESSES watch his every move.*) Your daughters have spent their evenings in an underground castle, beyond a shimmering lake--reached by a secret passageway through a forest of gold, silver and diamonds. They danced with twelve princes who were made captive through magic--as they tried to make me captive, this very night.

KING: (*Eyes narrowing.*) How do you come to know this?

MICHAEL: By means of a cloak given to me by an old

woman--a cloak which made me invisible, and able to follow.

KING: Have you any tangible proof of what you have seen?

MICHAEL: (*Behind ASHLEY, takes the chalice from her.*) The chalice which your oldest daughter holds. It came from there. (*Offers the chalice back to her; SHE swipes it from him with a glare.*)

KING: (*To the PRINCESSES.*) Is this true?

SARAH: (*Looks to the others; then, in a strong voice:*) Yes, Father. It is.

KING: And the rest of you?

THE PRINCESSES: Yes, Father.

KING: (*The anger beginning to well up.*) Very well. I promised the hand of one of my daughters to the man who solved the mystery, and I am a man of my word. But before you make your choice, son, I would like a few moments alone with these deceitful creatures. (*The PRINCESSES back off into a group, meekly, except for SARAH and ASHLEY. The KING takes an angry step toward them all--but is stopped by MICHAEL's voice.*)

MICHAEL: No, sir.

SARAH: Michael...

KING: What?

MICHAEL: (*Standing his ground.*) No. Sir.

KING: Do you know to whom you are talking?

MICHAEL: Yes, sir. A father who loves his daughters very much, and can't bring himself to tell them so. Who thinks that because they are almost grown, they no longer need to hear the words--unless concealed in a shout. (*Pause; HE turns to the Princesses.*) A man whose daughters love him very much, but must find their own way in the end. And yet, who still think that being true to yourself means being false to someone else--that because a father sheds no tears on the outside, he does not cry them on the inside. (*Pause.*) I have lost my own family--I know how it feels. If leaving you alone means helping you to lose yours, then no. I will not go. (*A long silence. The KING stands off, in thought, by the downstage bench, fingering the keys.*)

HOLLY: (*To ASHLEY.*) I think it's time for that talking you were going to do.

ASHLEY: Father... (*HE holds up his hand to stop her; she's silent.*)

KING: (*Quietly, as much to himself as to her.*) It's a strange thing. We promise that we will always remember how it felt to be young--and that seems to be the first thing we forget.

ASHLEY: (*Faint smile.*) You don't mean that you did something like this?

KING: No--of course not. (*Slight pause.*) I might have slipped out to battle a few dragons--maybe had a little singed armor to explain, but...dancing? Never. (*ASHLEY smiles. The KING smiles back, then is thoughtful again.*) This, ah...castle of yours...It must be very beautiful.

ASHLEY: (*Wistful.*) Yes. It was.

KING: Was?

ASHLEY: (*Simply.*) It's gone now.

KING: (*Genuinely.*) I'm sorry. (*Pause.*) I try to do what's best--truly. I'm sorry that I don't always see clearly what that is. How I miss the other pair of eyes that were my help...

ASHLEY (*Beginning to give way.*) So do I. (*A pause; ASHLEY and the KING look at each other, and embrace.*)

KING: Then...we must help each other. (*Steps back, and turns to the others; a bit of a pronouncement, but genuine.*) To you and your sisters, I give these keys. As an emblem of my trust, and love.

ASHLEY: (*Takes the keys, with a look around at the other PRINCESSES, then back to the KING.*) From me and my sisters, I give you this chalice. As an emblem of our respect, and love.

NICOLE: That was sooooooo beautiful... (*SHE rushes to embrace the KING; the other PRINCESSES follow in a group, except for SARAH, who stands with MICHAEL. After the KING has been mobbed:*)

LUCY: Wait a minute, Father: haven't you forgotten something?

KING: Hmmm?   (*LUCY indicates SARAH and MICHAEL.*) Yes, yes, of course. (*HE and ASHLEY set the keys and chalice on the bench. Formally, but with a twinkle in his eye.*) Michael, have you made your choice? (*Slowly, from somewhere, a dazzling figure enters. SHE bears a familiar resemblance to the OLD WOMAN, the MUSIC TEACHER, the LADY-IN-WAITING, and the CHAMBERMAID—but she is more beautiful than all of them. SHE wears the magic cloak, so we know that no one can see that she is, in fact, the spirit of THE QUEEN...*)

MICHAEL: I have.

KING: And who could that possibly be.

MICHAEL: (*With a smile.*) The Princess Sarah, Your Majesty.

KING: (*Genuinely looking at his daughter; takes her hand.*) With my blessings. (*General pleasure and excitement as they embrace, even ASHLEY looking on happily. THE QUEEN moves down to stand next to the KING—putting her hand on his shoulder, which he senses.*)

SARAH: Father...will you grant me a favor? (*No reply;

the KING is sensing a presence.) Father?
KING: Hmmm?
SARAH: A favor--if you would.
KING: Anything.
SARAH: There has never been dancing in the palace.
KING: (*Slight pause.*) Of course there has been.
SARAH: Not that I can remember.
KING: (*Quieter.*) No. Not since...It was before you were born.
SARAH: Then I think it's time we had it again. Don't you?
KING: (*Not sure.*) Dancing? (*The QUEEN makes a sign--and dance music begins out of nowhere.*)
THE PRINCESSES: Dancing! (*The KING looks up, baffled, then at SARAH--who takes his hand and ASHLEY's and puts them together. The KING and ASHLEY take the floor and lead off a dance--followed by SARAH and MICHAEL, who remain together, even as the KING changes partners to dance with the rest of his daughters. The music, bright and joyous, fills the room; the QUEEN stands watching for a moment, her family together again, and then drifts off. The dancing continues as the lights fade slowly, a single spotlight lingering on the chalice and keys before the stage is dark. The music plays on.*)

END OF PLAY

MUSIC NOTES

Depending on the style of production, just about any kind of music can be used to accompany the play--from Renaissance to Baroque to something with a more modern flavor. (Richard Jennings' original music for the first production combined Mediterranean influences with electronic sound to create a style that was both contemporary and exotic.) In general, music which lends itself to ballet-influenced dance is preferable. If the director chooses to include the choral singing in Scene 2, any appropriate song will do--from an authentic madrigal to any traditional folk melody. As for the underscoring during the climax of Scene 6, any sort of dramatic--even discordant--music could be used, whether stylistically similar to the rest of the music in the play or not. The fantasy world is collapsing, and the music and sound should reflect this.

SCENIC NOTES

The primary scenic note is: the simpler, the better. A unit set capable of serving for all locations, with minimal furniture or decoration changes (throne, banners, etc.), is best--with lighting doing as much work as possible. The original design utilized a castle-like structure with a multi-arched alcove upstage, and a "stone" floor downstage. A throne and banner indicated the throne room; a flowered trellis, the castle terrace. No beds at all appeared in the bedchamber. For the underground castle, gauze curtains were lowered in the arches; several Princesses danced behind them, holding darkly-costumed mannequins--lit just enough to give the illusion of dancing with partners. The downstage bench, which was not movable and was painted to look like carved stone, featured a hinged lid which could be opened in Scene 4, allowing for lights inside the bench to shine into the room as though from underground. This is one idea only; the princesses can make their "exit" through any available means--a wall, a curtain--with the dialogue adjusted as necessary.

CASTING NOTES

It is an understood convention of the play that the majority of the sisters are teenagers--even though this would be a real-life impossibility. When casting the Princesses, the actual ages of the performers is less important than the subtle differences in style, attitude, presence and--in some cases--maturity that mark them oldest to youngest. The adult roles may be played either by adults or by younger actors.

A Few Notes About The Princesses...

1. ASHLEY--Oldest, somewhat imperious, serious, possessed of complete regality--she's going to be the queen, and knows it, and wants everyone else to know it, too. She is completely sure of the rightness of her opinion, whether it's really right or not. Is not to be bothered with trifles.

2. CHELSEA--Second-oldest. In a tricky position: if you can't be queen, at least you can be the queen's Number One Assistant. On the other hand, she knows what it's like to be thought a lesser individual--and so she has more

compassion for the younger ones than her sister.   A sensitive, silent observer--and a better dancer than Ashley.

3. HOLLY--Smart, sensible, will tease for fun but not to hurt; content to let other people do whatever makes them happy, as long as they let her do the same. Perfectly secure in who she is, and doesn't feel she needs to explain it--but also savvy enough to know which way the wind is blowing, and go with it.

4. JESSI--The most beautiful--or at least, makes herself look so. Thoroughly self-conscious: every hair must be in place, every spangle on that dress must be shining and every male in the room must openly look at her first when she comes in. Tries to be what she thinks princes would want her to be if she could figure out what they're really like, which she can't. Most likely to be jealous.

5. JILL--Somewhat shy, bright, reluctant, probably better looking than Jessi but somehow always manages to make herself look plainer. She would be perfectly content to have a minor castle somewhere out in the provinces, with a lesser prince for a husband as long as he was a nice guy and treated her OK. Has a case of Lowered Expectations, which will probably be met. Feels just a little bit bad about defying Dad.

6. LILY--and--

7. LINDSAY--The Twins. They act alike, they walk alike, at times they even talk alike...[If you're not fortunate enough to have real twins, all that matters is the illusion.]

8. LUCY--This girl just wants to have fun. She's a Prince's Best Pal, because there aren't any expectations at all, aside from having a great time. Eventually she'll end up being the girl that they come to and say "I just wanted to tell you: I'm getting married", but who's thinking that far ahead?

9. MORGAN--Brooding. Something is going to go wrong, she just knows it. It really doesn't matter whether Dad finds out or not, since all existence is temporary--and dancing is certainly nice, but in the long run it doesn't change the fact that the universe is collapsing in on itself. The Princess most likely to be bound and gagged and tossed over a cliff by her sisters.

10. NICOLE--The Romantic. Every inch of life is an adventure, and every evening is going to be The Evening when the most perfect moon will light the most perfect forest and the most perfect music and the most perfect moments. And, if it doesn't happen, that's OK--there's always tomorrow night. Nicole would be in charge of choosing the Theme for the Castle Prom; her heart beats 27 beats a minute faster than any of her sisters.

11. SHANNON--The Gossip, the Giggler, the Tattler, the Whisperer. At her best at the dance with seven girls who all run into the bathroom together; tends to talk first and think much, much later...At the right time, she's exactly the person you want around. At other times, she's the one you wish would get a life. But it's always innocent, and easily forgiven.

12. SARAH--The Youngest Princess. Soft, natural beauty;

used to being passed over in the crowd for one of her flashier or more interesting sisters, and so she has learned to keep her own counsel. The flash of the outer world is intriguing, but more intriguing are the mysteries of her own heart, which keep nudging at her. Up to now, she's been hamstrung by the rules placed on her by others--but eventually she'll encounter someone out there who will surprise even herself, by inspiring her to follow that heart, even if her head doesn't totally understand why. And then one day, out for a walk and absorbed in her own musings about life and what it means, she saw this young man standing by the side of the road. And something clicked that had never clicked before...

*

www.ingramcontent.com/pod-product-compliance
Lightning Source LLC
Chambersburg PA
CBHW070401120726
47909CB00008B/2952